This book belongs to:

_____

This paperback edition first published in 2010 by Andersen Press Ltd.,
20 Vauxhall Bridge Road, London SW1V 2SA.
First published in Great Britain in 1969 by Blackie.
Published in Australia by Random House Australia Pty.,
Level 3, 100 Pacific Highway, North Sydney, NSW 2060.
Text copyright © John Yeoman, 1969.
Illustration copyright © Quentin Blake, 1969.
The rights of John Yeoman and Quentin Blake to be identified as the
author and illustrator of this work have been asserted by them in
accordance with the Copyright, Designs and Patents Act, 1988.
All rights reserved. Colour separated in Switzerland by Photolitho AG, Zürich.
Printed and bound in Malaysia by Tien Wah Press.

10   9   8   7   6   5   4

British Library Cataloguing in Publication Data available.

ISBN 978 1 84939 004 0

This book has been printed on acid-free paper

MIX
Paper from
responsible sources
FSC® C012700
www.fsc.org

The Bear's Water Picnic

John Yeoman   Quentin Blake

ANDERSEN PRESS

One fine spring day the pig, the squirrel, the hedge-hog and the hen were making their way to the big lake at the edge of the forest.

"Hurry up," said the pig. "We mustn't be late for the bear's water picnic." And when they reached the water, there was the bear, with a large picnic basket and two straw hats. "It's just the day for a water picnic," he called, as they ran up to him.

After they had all said hello to each other,
the bear showed them his special surprise –
a raft he had made. "Let's float out into
the middle of the lake and have a
nice quiet picnic in the
sun," he said.

Everyone was delighted. They all settled down
comfortably on the raft, and the bear gently pushed
them away from the shore with a long pole. The raft
glided smoothly over the blue water between the dark
green lily pads.

Soon they reached the middle of the lake. "Just the place for a picnic," the bear said, lifting the lid of the basket.

There was something for everyone:

acorns for the pig,

barley for the hen,

hazel nuts for the squirrel,

dead beetles for the hedgehog

and honeycomb for himself.

What's more, they all had a napkin with their initial on it to tie around their necks.

But no sooner had they started to eat their delicious
picnic than they heard a loud croaking noise.
"*Awrk, awrk*," it went. They put down their food
and looked over the side of the raft. And there, on a
lily pad, was a fat frog. "*Awrk, awrk*," he went again.
"What a terrible noise!" said the pig. "He'll spoil our
water picnic, if he goes on like that."

But that wasn't the worst of it. The hen pointed her wing at all the other lily pads. There was a frog sitting on each one, and they all started to go "*awrk, awrk*". "What a lovely day for a water picnic, *awrk, awrk*," they said. "May we join you?"

The bear carefully picked up the fat frog.
"We'd very much like to share our picnic with you,"
he said, "if only you would stop going *awrk, awrk*."
"We can't, *awrk, awrk*," said the frog cheerfully.
"In that case," said the bear with a sigh, "I think we
shall have to move on to a quieter part of the lake."
The friends set off again, leaving the noisy frogs
behind. They floated across the blue lake until
suddenly – without any warning – there was a great
bump, and they all fell over on their backs with their
legs in the air.

The animals quickly picked themselves up and peered over the edges of the raft to see what had happened.

"We're stuck!" wailed the hedgehog.

"We've hit a sandbank," said the pig, solemnly.

They took hold of the pole and pushed with all their might against the sandbank. The hen stood on the bear's head and shouted encouragement. "Push!" she squawked. "Push! Push!" But the raft wouldn't budge.

"We shall have to stay here until we are rescued," said the hen.

"That might be hours," said the squirrel.

"We might run out of food," sobbed the pig. And they all sat down, looking tired and miserable.

But the bear had an idea. "One of us must swim to the shore for help," he said brightly. But the shore was a long way away and when they tried the water, it was cold and deep. So the hedgehog rolled up into a ball, the hen put her head under her wing, and the squirrel curled up inside the picnic basket. The pig looked embarrassed and said, "Pigs can't swim."

"Like bears," said the bear, not quite truthfully.

Then the bear had another idea. "Perhaps the frogs will help us," he said. So they stood up and called for the frogs at the tops of their voices. And soon the cheerful frogs began to appear, *awrk-awrking* as they came. The animals all started to explain at once what had happened.

"That's easy, *awrk, awrk,*" said the fat frog, and all the frogs began to clamber onto the sandbank.

At a sign from the fat frog, they all jumped into the water and made an enormous wave, which lifted the raft away from the bank. "We're moving!" shouted the animals happily. "*Awrk, awrk,*" croaked the frogs.

As the raft drifted along, the grateful animals unpacked the hamper and offered to share their picnic food with the frogs. "No thank you very much," said the fat frog. "You see, your honeycomb attracts flies, and frogs like flies better than anything."

After the animals had eaten enough food and the frogs
had caught enough flies, the frogs began to sing their
"*awrk, awrk*" song again. But this time the animals
were so happy that they joined in.

As the sun began to set over the lake, the five animals and their frog friends drifted to the shore.

"Time to go home," said the bear, yawning contentedly, and they all said good-bye to each other.

"Come back soon for another water picnic, *awrk*, *awrk*," called the frogs.

And they all agreed they would.

Also by Quentin Blake

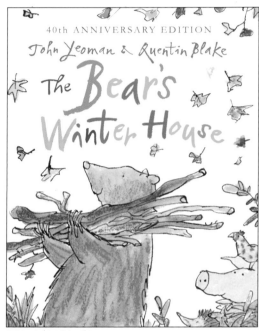

9781842709160

9781842709146

9781842708569

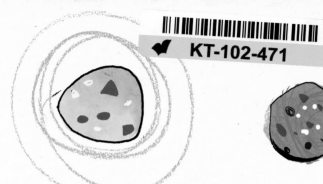

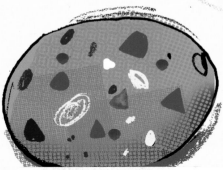

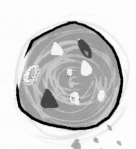

In memory of my mum – J.R.

For Dan x – C.E.

First published in Great Britain in 2014 by
Piccadilly Press, a Templar/Bonnier publishing company
Deepdene Lodge, Deepdene Avenue, Dorking, Surrey RH5 4AT
www.piccadillypress.co.uk

Designed by Simon Davis
Printed and bound in China by WKT
Colour reproduction by Dot Gradations

ISBN: 978 1 84812 402 8 (hardback)
ISBN: 978 1 84812 401 1 (paperback)

1 3 5 7 9 10 8 6 4 2

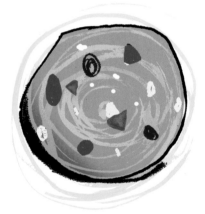

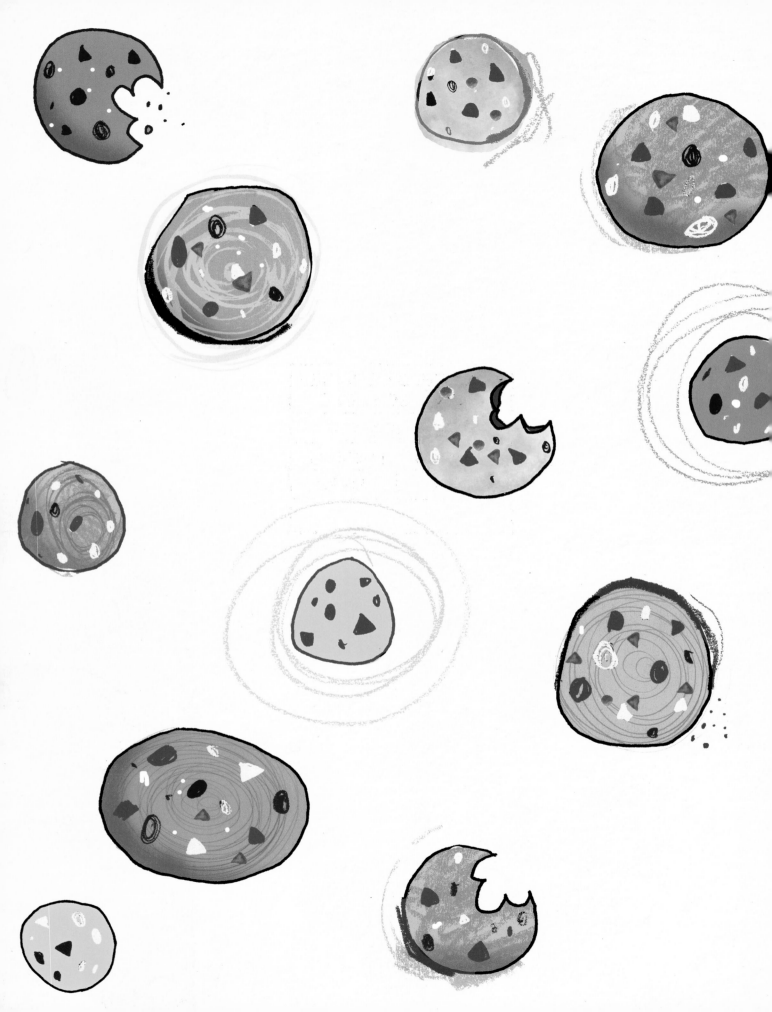

The Last Chocolate Chip Cookie

Jamie Rix

Illustrated by Clare Elsom

Piccadilly

There was one chocolate chip cookie left on the plate, so I leaned across the table and took it.

"Jack," gasped my mum.
"Where are your manners? Offer the
last chocolate chip cookie to
everyone else first."

"EVERYONE else?" I said.
"EVERYONE else," she insisted.

So I put the last chocolate chip cookie
in my pocket and did as I was told.

I offered it
to my brother,
but he didn't want it.

I offered it to my dad, but he didn't want it.

I offered it to Gran,

and even to the cat,

but they didn't want it.

So I offered the last chocolate chip cookie to my teacher,

the
window
cleaner,

the bus driver,

I went all round the world and offered
it to anyone I could find, including
a Mexican marzipan-maker with a moustache.

But no one wanted it.

So I took the last chocolate chip cookie
into space and offered
it to an alien.

But the alien didn't want to eat
the last chocolate chip cookie . . .

He wanted to eat ME!

"Splagly!" gasped his alien mumma.
"Where are your manners?
Offer the human being to everyone else first."

"EVERYONE else?" he said.

"EVERYONE else," she insisted.

So Splagly put me in his pocket and did as he was told.

He offered me to his brotter, his daddle, his grin-gran,

the cattamog, his tin teacher, the window wiper,

the spacebus pilot and the fang-filler.

He flew all round the universe and offered me
to any alien he could find . . .
including a four-eyed
Bogly Marsh-masher.

But no one wanted me . . .

. . . until he arrived back on Earth

and
offered
me to
my mum.

"Yes, I would like him, please," she said.
"It's lovely to meet an alien with such good manners."

I told my mum that I'd offered the last chocolate chip cookie to everyone else but no one had wanted it.

"Then you can eat it," she said.
"It will taste twice as delicious now that you've been so polite."

As I took it out of my pocket I was drooling.

I'd waited a long time to eat the last chocolate chip cookie.

I took a bite . . .

IT TASTED LIKE

CARBOARD

GUNK-GLOOP

WITH HAIRS

ON IT!

Do YOU want the last chocolate chip cookie?

LAST CHOCOLATE CHIP COOKIE RECIPE:

YOU NEED:

175g butter
225g caster sugar
2 x eggs
350g x self raising flour
100g x chocolate chips

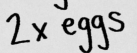

ALSO:
LARGE BAKING TRAY
MIXING BOWL
ELECTRIC WHISK

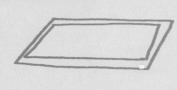

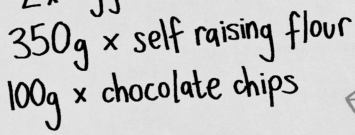

GET COOKING: *

Pre-heat oven to 180°
Add all ingredients to bowl and mix well
Spoon dollops of the mixture onto baking tray
(grease the tray first and leave lots of room between each one)
Bake in oven for 15-20 minutes until golden

EAT AND ENJOY AND
DON'T LEAVE THEM
IN YOUR POCKET TILL
THEY'RE MOULDY!

* get an adult to help with the oven!

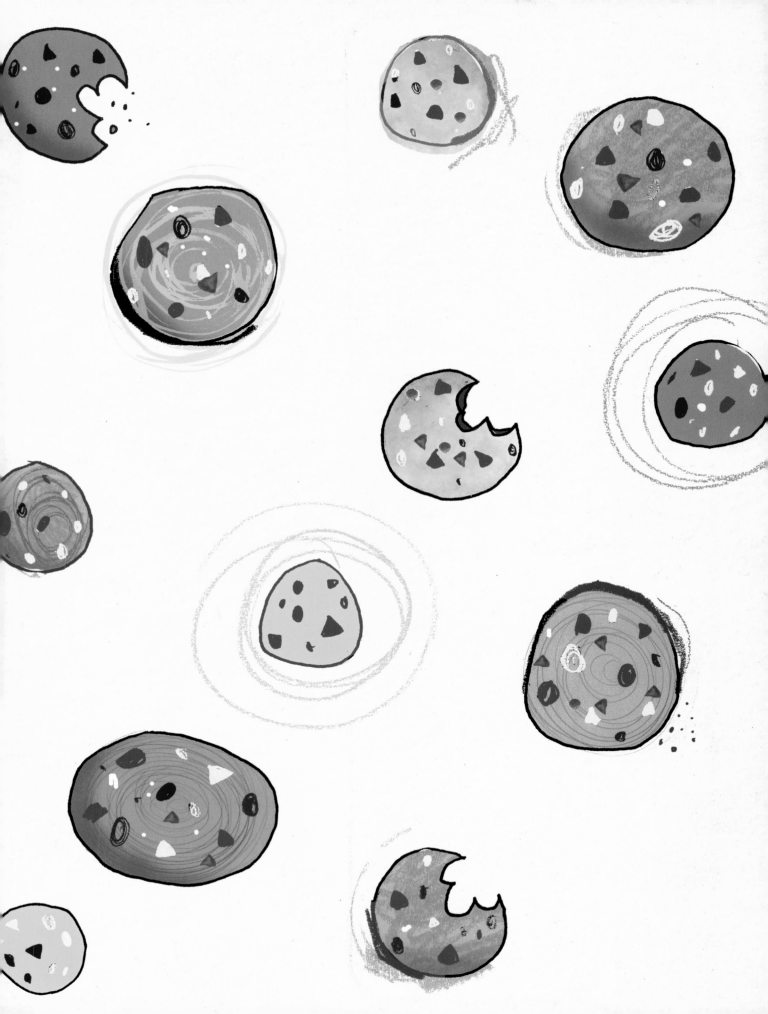